To glacier lovers everywhere. —Liz
To my favorite Rocks. —Alice

Glacier
on the
Move

Hi, I'm an ice worm. Turn the page to learn all about my favorite glacier, Flo.

Written by Elizabeth Rusch
Illustrated by Alice Brereton

WEST
MARGIN
PRESS

Hello, my name is Flo.

It might not look like it, but I FLOW.
I'm like a river of ice, always on the move.

I was born during the Little Ice Age,
but I'm not staying little for long.
I have plans, **BIG** plans.
I'm heading for the ocean.
I can't wait to see the sea!

Many glaciers formed during the Little Ice Age, a cool period hundreds of years ago.

Yahoo! Snow day. I bet you thought I was made from frozen water like an ice cube.

I'm actually made from snow.
So pile it on!
I'm going to need tons to reach the sea!

As snow piles on a glacier, the weight presses air out, compacting the snow into dense ice.

It takes 10 years for 10 feet of snow to become 1 foot of glacial ice.

Gotta hang out while
my ice builds up.
It's summertime,
so I'm a little sweaty,
but not too bad.

Still chillin'.

Waiting.

For a glacier to grow, more snow has to fall in winter than melts in summer.

It takes hundreds, even thousands, of years for glaciers to grow, shrink, and move.

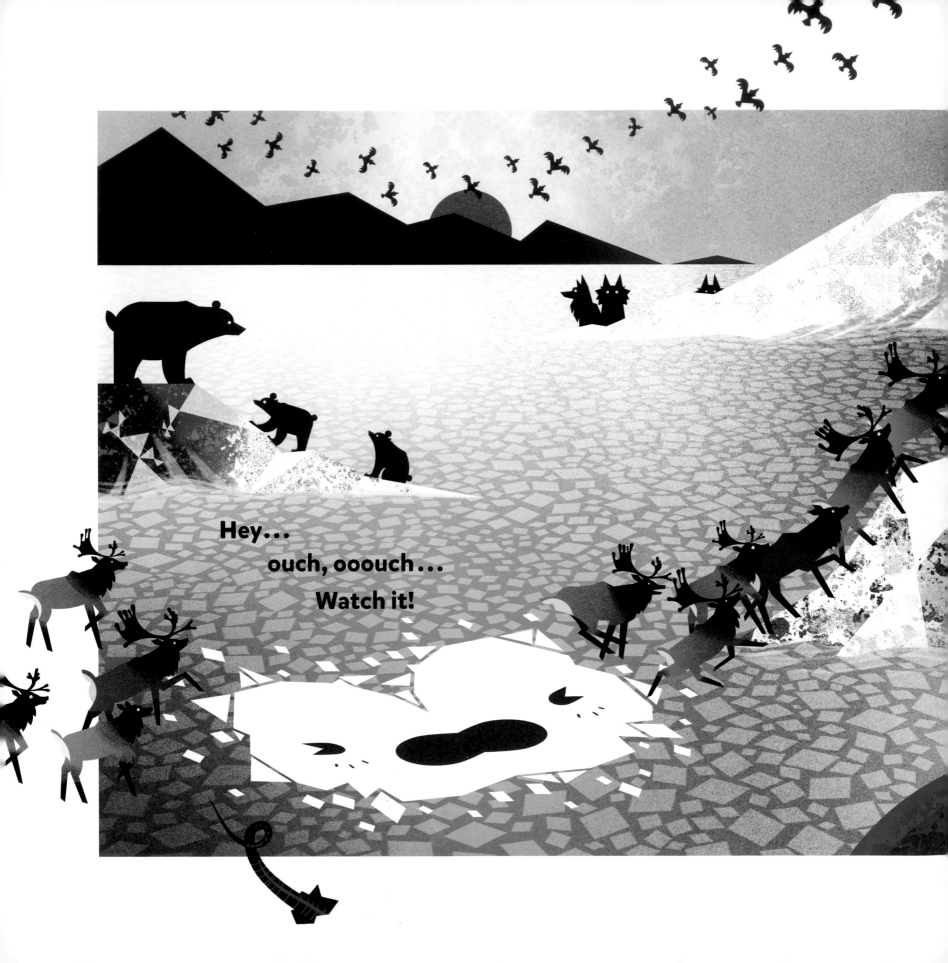

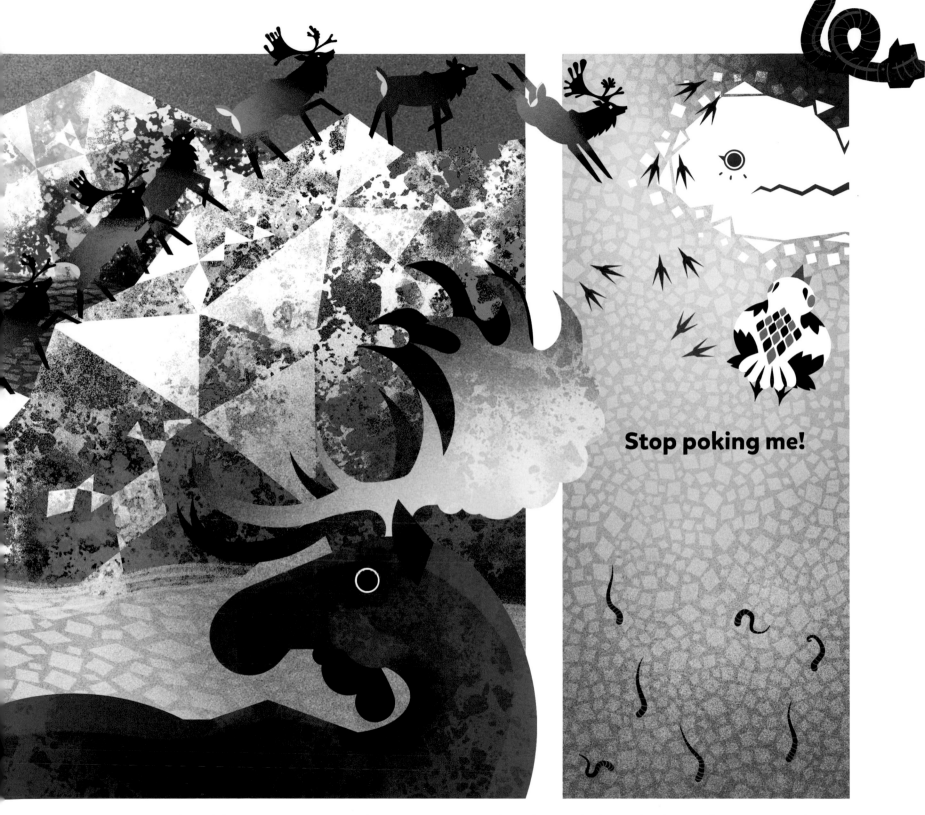

Stop poking me!

While many creatures visit glaciers, ice worms are the only animals that make glaciers their permanent home.

Glaciers move because gravity tugs the ice downhill.

Phew, it's about time. I'm finally ready to drop off this cliff.

A glacier on a steep hill picks up speed. But it still moves slowly—less than 3 feet a year.

Galloping Glacier,
here I Goooooooo!

Dragging rocks and boulders along, glaciers carve deep grooves into the ground called striations.

I'm feeling groovy and making my mark…

Glaciers carry dirt that can form dark stripes in the ice.

... Woohoo!
Check out my racing stripes.

Watch out forest, here I come.

CRUnCH! CRaCK!

Glaciers can crush trees—even whole forests—in their paths.

Sometimes a glacier surges forward, moving up to 10 times its normal speed.

CRASH!

Oops, sorry, trees.

Valley glaciers flow down between mountains.

Ugh, it's really tight
through this valley.
Got … to … squeeeeeze
my way through.

Glaciers look blue because glacial ice absorbs red and yellow light, but reflects blue.

Uh-oh, another big rock in the way. Can't let a little ol' boulder stop me from reaching the sea.

Maybe if I melt a little,

A glacier pressing against something can melt the ice, so the water drips around it and refreezes.

I can get around it...

Top layers can stay frozen and crack under pressure, forming deep crevasses.

Feels good to finally

s t r e t c h h h h h

out a bit.

AHHHhhhhhhhh!

When valley glaciers pour onto flat land, they fan out into piedmont glaciers.

So close! Just
need
to
inch a...

little
farther...

A glacier that touches the sea is called a tidewater glacier.

Hurray! The sea—the shining sea!
I made it. And it's more beautiful
than I ever imagined.
I wonder why the
water looks so milky?

Glaciers can grind rocks into powder, called rock flour, which turns water milky gray.

Harbor seals move onto tidewater glaciers to give birth and nurse their pups.

Huh, it feels kinda warm around here.

Water carries heat 25 times better than land, so glacial ice melts faster in it.

PING CRaCKle FizzzzzzZZ

When a glacier melts, the air trapped in bubbles can explode noisily.

As warm water melts the bottom layers of the glacier, heavy overhanging ice falls, or calves.

I'm breaking up!

I gotta get away from this warm water.
Retreat!

SPLASH!

Look, Flo made icebergs!

A retreating glacier often leaves behind piles of debris called moraines.

Sigh. Had to leave my awesome rock collection behind.
But check out what's growing on it.

Moss and lichen take root, seeds blow in, and soon shrubs and trees begin to grow here.

Don't get too cozy,
'cause here comes the snow again.

Galloping Glacier, here I goooo!

I hope Flo keeps growing. She is, after all, home sweet home!

GLACIERS OF THE WORLD

◆ About 10 percent of land in the world is covered with glaciers.

◆ Glaciers can be found on all of the world's continents, even Africa.

◆ Glaciers hold three-quarters of the world's fresh water.

◆ If all glacial ice melted, seas would rise more than 250 feet (75 meters). That's as high as a 25-story building!

◆ Alaska has the most glaciers in the United States, roughly 100,000.

◆ Glaciers can also be found in California, Colorado, Idaho, Montana, Nevada, Oregon, Washington, and Wyoming.

GLACIERS AND GLOBAL CLIMATE CHANGE

For the past 100 years, glaciers around the globe, especially on mountains, have been retreating. While some retreat cycles occur naturally, the current rapid retreat of glaciers is due primarily to human activity. The burning of fossils fuels (gas, oil, and coal) is warming the planet at faster rates than ever before. As the planet's climate warms, more moisture falls as rain and less as snow. Warmer summers mean faster melting. More ice is melting than is being made on most of the world's glaciers, so they are receding, some quite rapidly.

To help, do all you can to reduce the burning of fossil fuels: walk, ride your bike, or carpool when possible; eat less meat; turn off lights and electronics that you are not using; turn off the water when you brush your teeth or soap up in shower; reuse and recycle everything you can. Our planet, glaciers, and ice worms are counting on you!

All about meeeeeee!

OUR SCIENCE EXPERTS: ICE WORMS

There really are worms that live their entire lives in glaciers. Ice worms are segmented worms, similar to the common earthworm. Usually under an inch long (1–3 centimeters), very thin, and in brown, black, or blue colors, these creatures have anti-freeze in their tissues that allows them to thrive at freezing temperatures.

Ice worms are surprisingly agile. They use small bristles outside their bodies to grip and push through ice crystals—sometimes moving as fast as 10 feet an hour. At dawn and dusk, they often wriggle to the surface to feed on algae and pollen. But if the air temperature rises above or below freezing, the worms burrow back into the glacial ice, where temperatures stay a steady 32°F (0°C). Ice worms are so well adapted to glacial ice that if they face temperatures just 5°F above freezing, their bodies liquefy.

READ MORE

Alaska Glacier Directory: library.alaska.gov/asp/Alaska_Glaciers.html

Alaska's Glaciers Frozen in Motion by Katherine Hocker (Alaska Geographic, 2006).

All About Glaciers/National Snow and Ice Data Center: nsidc.org/cryosphere/glaciers

Glaciers of the American West: glaciers.research.pdx.edu/

Ice Worms: alaskacenters.gov/explore/culture/ice-worms; summitpost.org/exploring-the-mystery-of-glacier-ice-worms/835795

NASA's Global Climate Change website: climate.nasa.gov

USGS Glaciers and Climate Project: https://www2.usgs.gov/landresources/lcs/glacierstudies/

Library of Congress Cataloging-in-Publication
Data is on file

ISBN: 9781513262307 (hardbound)
       9781513262314 (e-book)

Proudly distributed by Ingram Publisher Services

Printed in China
23 22 21 20 19 1 2 3 4 5

Published by West Margin Press

WEST
MARGIN
PRESS

WestMarginPress.com

WEST MARGIN PRESS
Publishing Director: Jennifer Newens
Marketing Manager: Angela Zbornik
Editor: Olivia Ngai
Design & Production: Rachel Lopez Metzger